RIDLEY BLUEFOX

AND THE
FLYING FISH OF
FORTUNE FALLS

Ridley Bluefox and the Flying Fish of Fortune Falls
Text © 2007 Carrie Percy

Published by Lobster Press™
1620 Sherbrooke Street West, Suites C & D
Montréal, Québec   H3H 1C9
Tel. (514) 904-1100 • Fax (514) 904-1101 • www.lobsterpress.com

Publisher: Alison Fripp
Editors: Alison Fripp & Meghan Nolan
Editorial Assistants: Katie Scott and Olga Zoumboulis
Cover Illustration: Sandra Lamb
Graphic Design & Production: Tammy Desnoyers

We acknowledge the financial support of the Government of Canada through the Book Publishing Industry Development Program (BPIDP) for our publishing activities.

The Canada Council | Le Conseil des Arts
for the Arts | du Canada

We acknowledge the support of the Canada Council for the Arts for our publishing program.

Library and Archives Canada Cataloguing in Publication

Percy, Carrie, 1975-
     Ridley Bluefox and the flying fish of Fortune Falls / Carrie Percy.

ISBN-13: 978-1-897073-59-9
ISBN-10: 1-897073-59-3

     I. Title.

PS8631.E73R53 2007   jC813'.6   C2006-905177-1

Printed and bound in Canada.

For Gavin, who taught me that it is possible to talk about fishing for hours and hours (and hours).

– Carrie Percy

RIDLEY BLUEFOX

AND THE
FLYING FISH OF
FORTUNE FALLS

written by
Carrie Percy

Lobster Press ™

Look for "fishnotes" 🐟 throughout the book
to learn the meaning of certain words.

PROLOGUE

RIDLEY BLUEFOX HAD never met a fish he couldn't catch. Ridley Bluefox had never even heard of a fish he couldn't catch. He could catch anything. He even caught fish he didn't want to catch. At twelve years of age, Ridley was already a very famous fisherman. And it is a good thing he was, because fishing is really all he did and all he wanted to do.

It all started four years ago when he landed himself on the cover of *Fishin' Fabulous* magazine at the tender age of eight. He'd been on a family vacation to the island of Wangodo when he had caught the magnificent, yet elusive, Pollo Pollo with a leftover shish kebab stick from dinner. In fact, that trip to Wangodo was a turning point in Ridley's life because it opened him up to the exciting world of fishing. Ever since, fishing was the only thing he ever thought about. All of his school projects were about fish. Every book he read was about fish. The only television shows he would watch were about fish.

But it was the fame of being interviewed and photographed that really lit a fire in Ridley's belly. Every time he came home from an adventure with a fish the world had never seen or with a catch that no other fisherman could manage to make, he ended up on the cover of *Fishin'*

Fabulous. The interviewers loved him for his crazy fishing tales that always seemed to end in a magnificent catch. The photographers loved his proud smile and the exotic fish he held up for pictures. The magazines always sold out when Ridley was on the front cover. Fishermen all around the world couldn't believe that he was able to bring home fish that no one else could catch.

Ridley was tall for his twelve years, with a lanky frame. His skin was deeply tanned from all of the time he spent outdoors, and his dark brown mop of hair was always covered by a fishing hat decorated with his most successful fishing lures. Ridley loved the media attention that his miraculous, adventurous catches got him. More than anything else, it was the desire for this fame that pushed him deeper into the world of fishing.

Once he had kebabbed the Pollo Pollo, Ridley could not get enough. He had gone on to catch great trophies in the world of fishing and graced a good many more front covers of *Fishin' Fabulous* too. He'd been on fourteen magazine covers in the last four years! At home his room was full of stuffed and mounted fish from exotic locales the world over.

But this story is not about any of those accomplishments or any of the stuffed fish on his wall. This is the story of the flying fish of Fortune Falls - fish that are conspicuously absent from the walls and halls of the Bluefox home.

Fortune Falls is nestled in one of the tropical jungles of

Pingu Ma, and it is one of the more stunning places on earth. It is a very hard place to reach, and not many people have heard of it. Now, it may seem strange to you that Ridley's parents had no problem with their young son gallivanting around the globe to places like Pingu Ma. But that is because you don't know the Bluefox family. Ridley comes from a long line of explorers and adventurers. Take, for example, his great-great-granduncle Bartholomew Bluefox. This man was known as "The Terror of the South Seas." He was a ruthless explorer for whom no territory was too wild. He discovered the ancient city of Navea and retired from the high seas to be an advisor to his Imperial Majesty, the King.

Then, of course, there is Ridley's father and mother, Engelbert and Eugenia Bluefox. Engelbert grew up in a secret druid village and has been a leading world authority on the subject of rune stones since he was sixteen years of age. His prize possession is an ancient rune stone that he won in a battle against a Celtic alchemist he discovered hiding in an underground limestone cave.

Eugenia climbed Kilimanjaro at the age of fourteen. She lived with the emperor penguins in the Antarctic for a year when she was sixteen and married Ridley's father on the shores of the Amazon in her eighteenth year. They honeymooned in the Antilles .

Druid: a member of an ancient Celtic priesthood.
Rune: a mysterious symbol from an ancient Germanic alphabet that has supposed magical powers.
Celtic: a group of early European people from the British Isles; their customs, language, and religion.
Alchemist: a person who studies medieval chemical science and philosophy.
Kilimanjaro: a mountain in Tanzania, which is in eastern Africa.
Antilles: a group of islands located in the Caribbean Sea.

From the day Ridley was born, Engelbert and Eugenia took Ridley wherever they went. Whether it was diving for sunken treasure off the coast of Zanzibar ꙮ, living amongst the Bucca tribe, or crossing the Gobi ꙮ desert on camels, the Bluefoxes did it all as a family. So it came as no surprise to Engelbert and Eugenia when Ridley found his own passion. (However, they were surprised that he chose fish.) And because his parents were of the eccentric exploring type, they could hardly object when their only son turned out to be one of the same. Truth be told, the Bluefoxes were delighted that their son had inherited the family sense of adventure. They always prepared him the best they could for his travels, making sure he had his passport, money in a variety of currencies, a compass, good equipment, and contact information for friends of the Bluefox family who lived around the world.

When Ridley came home one day, talking about the flying fish of Fortune Falls in Pingu Ma, Engelbert and Eugenia Bluefox knew it was time to get ready for another one of Ridley's adventures. Pingu Ma is located in the South Pacific, making it both an exotic and remote location. They would have to prepare their son well for this particular journey.

Zanzibar: an island off the coast of Tanzania, Africa.
Gobi: a desert in central Asia.

CHAPTER 1

RIDLEY FIRST HEARD of Pingu Ma while he and his friends had been on a trip up in the wilds of Northern Ontario. Well, actually, he wasn't exactly on a fishing trip at the time, but rather on the way home from a trip. Ridley had convinced his older cousin Bert to drive a group of them up to Algonquin Park to go hiking, canoeing, and camping. Ridley's friends Wayne and Brian and his cousin Bert did all of those things during the trip. Ridley, of course, did nothing but fish.

On the way home, Ridley asked Bert to pull the van over to the side of a dirt road. He wanted to investigate a bait and tackle shop that he had never noticed before.

"Funny, but I am sure that we didn't pass this place on the way up. How could that be? I'll just check it out real quick. Wayne and Brian are sleeping anyway. Okay Bert?" Ridley asked.

"We're already stopped, so you may as well go and take a look. But I don't know why you would want to buy anything. Our trip is over!" Bert said. He was used to his younger cousin's obsession with fishing by now, but you could tell he still thought it was a weird thing to be so crazy about.

"I'll be quick," Ridley assured Bert as he climbed out of the van. "The guys'll never even know I was gone." And off he went 'cause the world knew that Ridley Bluefox couldn't pass by a fishing shop without peeking his head inside.

The store was dusty and musty and downright dirty. Ridley peered through the gloomy light and spied a thin and crooked old man hunched over in a lawn chair beside the only shelf in the store. Now, we all know that stores usually have many shelves, full of many, many things. So you can see why Ridley found it odd that this bait and tackle shop had one lonely little shelf and one lonely little old man. As he approached the man, he found it even stranger that the only shelf in the place held up only one box.

"Excuse me, old man, but what kind of bait and tackle shop is this?" Ridley inquired. "I see only one shelf and only one box. Where are your worms? Where are your leeches? Where are your lures, your bobbers, your waterproof breeches ?"

"Ah," said the man, with a gleam in his eye, "but you have all of that and more in your van, so why should I sell these things to you? I will sell you something you haven't got. Something you've never heard of - bait for a flying fish that you'll never catch!"

"That's ridiculous and that is absurd. There is nothing that I can't catch!" said Ridley. "You sit up and listen, you crooked old man! I'm Ridley Bluefox! I've caught Bunhonmucks, Persisskins, and Subahohives."

 **Breeches**: pants

"Of course you have. But flying fish are different, don't 'cha know! Especially the ones from Fortune Falls," croaked the old man with a sideways grin.

"What do you mean *different*? I'm Ridley Bluefox! Don't you know who I am? I've been on magazine covers for catching all sorts of exotic fish!" Ridley was disappointed that this crooked old man didn't seem to recognize him.

"I'm telling you, boy, you've never caught anything like this. I'll bet you don't even know where Fortune Falls is, do ya?" the old man said as he picked up the box of bait and shook it at Ridley, tempting him to take it.

"Of course I know where Fortune Falls is!" Ridley lied with a straight face. He wasn't going to let this ridiculous man make a fool of him.

"Oh really?" the old man said and raised his eyebrows in surprise. He set the box down on the counter. "Well, I must be wrong then and you must be right, Mr. Ridley Bluefox. I guess you won't be needing this special bait if you already know all about Fortune Falls."

"You guessed right, old man! There's nothing here I need!" Ridley turned on his heel and stomped out of the dusty shop. He marched all the way out to the van, reached for the door handle, and then stopped.

"I can't believe it," he sighed. "This is embarrassing, but I must have that bait!" Gritting his teeth, he turned back to the shop. Ridley marched over, opened the screen door, and barged through. The old man's eyes were gleaming with pleasure, and he tried to hide the smile on his face as he watched Ridley re-enter the shop. Ridley snatched up the box of flying fish bait, tossed some crumpled bills on the counter, marched back out of the store, and climbed into the van. He slammed his door shut in a huff, mumbling to himself, "A fish I can't catch? We'll see about that!"

"What'd ya get?" asked Bert.

"Never mind!" Ridley grumbled through clenched teeth. "Let's just go."

An hour or so later, Ridley was still miffed by the crooked old man's insinuation that somewhere on this planet there was a fish he couldn't catch (ha!), when Brian and Wayne began to wake up. Peering out of the van windows, they asked,

"Where are we?"

"Are we almost home?"

"I'm hungry."

"Let's stop for lunch."

So stop for lunch they did. While they stuffed back slices of pepperoni pizza and root beers, Ridley Bluefox told his friends about the old man and the dusty, dingy bait shop where he had convinced Bert to stop.

"I didn't see a shop along that road!" Wayne said. He sounded a bit offended that no one had woken him up.

"That is kind of strange. We were on the same road on the way up to our camping site, weren't we?" Brian added.

"Yeah, we were," Bert said. "We were probably talking

 Insinuation: to suggest something in an artful or indirect way.

or something and we missed it, that's all. Anyway, who cares about that? What's in the box?" he asked.

Ridley continued his griping and grumbling about how rude it was for the man to suggest that he, Ridley Bluefox, couldn't catch a fish, until Bert shoved a slice of pizza into Ridley's mouth to stop him from complaining.

"Get on with it already, Ridley!" Bert insisted.

So Ridley opened the box he had bought. It was a plain white cardboard box with strange red designs on the outside and folded flaps on top. Actually, it looked a lot like a take-out box from a Chinese food restaurant - more likely to hold chicken chow mein than bait for the flying fish of Fortune Falls.

Inside, there was a folded piece of paper. It felt thick and wrinkly between Ridley's fingers as he removed it. He set the paper aside and looked into the bottom of the box. Inside were five pink and yellow striped caterpillars squashed together. At least they resembled caterpillars. They looked like furry little logs, more fat than they were long. Ridley shook the box gently back and forth, but the caterpillar logs did not move. He reached in with one finger and poked at the fattest caterpillar, but there was no response. Ridley leaned his ear down to the opening of the little cardboard box and heard a small sawing sound. It sounded as if the tiniest lumberjack in all the world was sawing down the tiniest tree from the tiniest forest. It was the tiniest sawing sound Ridley had ever heard.

"I think they're snoring!" Ridley exclaimed as he showed his friends the contents of the box. "They must be sleeping!"

"What are they?" Wayne asked, sniffing at the contents of the box.

"How would I know?" Ridley responded in a grumpy voice and snatched the box back. He felt as if he should be able to explain the strange contents of the box, but he really had no idea what they were. He'd never seen fish bait like this in all his life!

"Maybe it says on that piece of paper you're holding," Wayne suggested.

"Yeah, check out the paper!" Brian suggested as he reached for it.

"Don't touch that, Brian! You'll get grease all over it!" Ridley warned as he closed the top flaps of his box, covering the snoring pink and yellow caterpillars, and reached for the paper. It felt old, as if it had been in the box for quite some time. Ridley unfolded the thick cream-colored paper and smoothed out the lines with his hands.

It was a map! It looked like an ancient treasure map, the kind they have in pirate movies. It was drawn in thick black ink, and all of the words were written in a fancy, old looking script. There in front of him was a detailed drawing of an island. The map was labeled "The Island of Fortuna," and down in the left-hand corner of the island was a flamboyantly marked X. Above the X was the name

"Fortune Falls." Ridley scanned the map as his friends peered over his shoulder.

"Wow!" said Bert.

"No way!" exclaimed Brian in surprise.

"It's a treasure map!" breathed Wayne.

As his friends stared over his shoulder, Ridley traced the outline of the Island of Fortuna and let out a long, low whistle. He scanned the rest of the paper and found a note written at the bottom of the page:

He who gazes upon these words,
Now heed the warning written here
The flying fish of Fortune Falls,
Have not been caught for many a year

The only man to catch such a fish,
Tears of joy he cried
So mighty and so many tears,
He dried right up and died

These fish you seek cannot be caught,
Your prize for trying will be naught.

"What are ya gonna do with it?" Wayne whispered.

"Ah, it's probably just a joke, a waste of money, but he got me good, that old man did! He really had me going." Ridley laughed as he folded the map and placed it back in the box with the snoring caterpillars.

"All right then. Come on guys, let's get back on the road," Bert suggested. They cleaned up, left the restaurant, and got back in the van. Bert hadn't been driving very long before Wayne and Brian fell asleep again, but not Ridley. He was wide awake, thinking about the message written at the bottom of the map. *"These fish you seek cannot be caught."* The words were ringing through his mind, challenging his skills as a fisherman. He had stored the cardboard box safely in his backpack when the others weren't looking, because secretly Ridley wasn't so sure it was all just a hoax. He was curious about the flying fish of Fortune Falls. He decided that when he got home, he'd have to find out more about The Island of Fortuna.

CHAPTER 2

BY THE TIME Bert dropped him off at home, Ridley was burning with questions. He ran into the house and found his parents in the den drinking tea, waiting for his safe return. Ridley immediately launched into his questions. Had they ever heard of this place? And what about these flying fish? It turns out that his father had heard of The Island of Fortuna, but he didn't know much about it. Engelbert told Ridley that Fortuna Island is part of a larger island called Pingu Ma that is somewhere in the South Pacific.

His father knew all about geography, but neither his father nor his mother were big fans of fish, so they didn't know much about ichthyology . It was obvious that Ridley had already decided that this was going to be his next big fishing expedition, so his parents suggested that he start by taking a trip to the local library. He was going to need to do some research in order to learn about the flying fish of Fortune Falls.

The next day, Ridley headed for the library. His plan was to look up information on Pingu Ma. With any luck, he would find mention of the flying fish.

Ridley's local library was a rather old and decrepit place. It was attached to the town's Museum of Natural

Ichthyology: the scientific study of fish.

History (Ridley had never visited either place). Following directions from the museum security guard, Ridley descended the cracked front steps, noticing how the moss was breaking the cement apart bit by little bit, and rounded the side of the building. There he saw a hanging wooden sign with the words "Public Library" and a thick black arrow pointing straight down. Below the sign there was a stone staircase cut into the ground. Ridley walked four steps down, turned right to another four steps down, and found himself at a wooden door that was propped open by a large stone.

"Come on in then, if you're going to," Ridley heard a voice call. "But leave the door open behind you there, if you don't so very much mind. I'm giving the periodicals - a good airing out today."

Ridley stepped through the doorway and ran right into a newspaper – smack in the face, as if it were suspended in mid air! The musty smell of old newsprint filled his nostrils as he glanced up and realized the room had been strung with makeshift clotheslines. Hanging from the clotheslines, which upon closer inspection appeared to be made of dental floss, were newspapers and magazines of all types and varieties. A quick scan of the room revealed the *London Examiner*, the *Denver Daily*, *Cat and Mouse Monthly*, *Knitting for Nitwits*, and Ridley's personal favorite, *Fishin' Fabulous*.

He was startled as the front page of the *Denver Daily* slid abruptly to the left to reveal a little man with a surpris-

---

 Periodical: a newspaper, magazine, or journal that is published on a regular basis.

ingly large red mustache. "Can't keep your periodicals too fresh, you know," the man said as he smiled, and in doing so, revealed a row of long, rather crowded looking teeth. One glance let Ridley know that the man had recently eaten spinach, and he couldn't help thinking that perhaps this little man with the big mustache could have saved some dental floss for himself.

The man turned on the heel of a badly scuffed brown leather loafer and toddled toward the front desk. He climbed up to sit on a stool behind the desk, crossed one leg over the other, and said, "Now, what can Pedro, that's me, and the public library do for you on this fine day?"

"I am doing some research about a place in the South Pacific called Pingu Ma. I thought you might have some information about it," said Ridley.

"Pingu Ma, Pingu Ma ..." Pedro tapped his forehead with his index finger as he thought about Ridley's request. "Never heard of the place myself. What you need is our mapping department. My brother Pondro will be able to help you, of course. *Pondro! Pondrooooooooo!*" Pedro leaned forward on his stool to get closer to Ridley and said, "He's probably asleep. He has a bit of a problem with that. Falls asleep for no good reason at all. It is very odd, but it happens to him all the time. That's why we put him way back in the map room. That way, he doesn't fall asleep on someone while he's checking their books out. That would be awfully rude, don't you think?"

"*Umm*, yeah, I guess so," Ridley answered. Falling asleep uncontrollably did sound odd, but the little man right in front of him, with a smile full of spinach, seemed a tad odd himself.

Pedro slipped off of his stool and gestured for Ridley to follow as he walked toward the back of the library. As they wandered through the stacks of books, Ridley realized how huge the library was. It was a long and wide hallway filled floor to ceiling with books of all imaginable sorts.

They finally reached the back wall and faced a tall wooden door. "The Map Room" was stenciled in faded gold lettering on the door's glass window. Pedro rapped on the door and pushed it wide open. Inside was a room that was wallpapered in various maps of Alaska. Everywhere Ridley looked, there was Alaska, except for directly in front of him. There, he saw a rickety old desk over which was slumped a little man with a surprisingly large red mustache. Pedro walked up to who must have been the slumbering Pondro, leaned over his ear, and yelled one last time, *Pooooonnnnndrooooo!*"

Pondro jumped up from his sleep so fast that he fell right off his chair and hit the floor with a thud. He climbed back onto his chair quick as a wink, yelling, "I'm up! I'm up!"

Ridley glanced from one brother to the other. Being a bit odd wasn't the only thing they had in common. They were identical! Seeing the twins together was more than a little peculiar – one standing upright, a smile on his face, his hands clasped behind his back, and the other sitting up at his desk, rubbing his eyes and yawning loudly.

"This young man here is in need of some of your maps. Try to stay awake long enough to help him," Pedro shouted. And with that declaration, the more alert of the two mustached brothers strode back through the book stacks toward the front of the library.

"Well, well. What can Pondro, that's me, and the map room do for you?" Pondro asked, wiping his face vigorously with his hands, as one is wont to do when one first wakes up.

"I'm looking for a map of a place called Pingu Ma. It's in the South Pacific somewhere ... well, that is, if it does really exist," Ridley explained with more than a little uncertainty in his voice.

"Well, well, looking for Pingu Ma, are you? You are a rare breed indeed. Most don't even know of its existence. I, of course, do. Map men of my caliber must know of Pingu Ma. It is a most unusual island. Well, well, p-p-*Pinguuuu* ... ah, here it is," Pondro mumbled as he flipped through a card catalogue. He pulled out the file card he'd located and slid the drawer shut with a puff of dust. "Follow me, if you please," he called over his shoulder as he ambled toward the back of the room.

The maps were housed in what amounted to a giant closet. Pondro pulled open the double doors, and inside hung a tightly packed row of maps. Each one was pinned to its own hanger and tagged for identification.

"It's color-coded, you see. My idea, of course. Green hangers for Asia, royal blue for Europe, red for North America ... ah yes, aquamarine ... the South Pacific. Here we are p-p-p-*Pinguuuu*, here it is, Pingu Ma!" Pondro produced the map with a flourish and carried it to a large table.

It was a very old map by the looks of it. The fold creases had worn away into holes at some points, and the paper had yellowed with age. But it was surely one of the most interesting maps that Ridley had ever had the pleasure of seeing. Pingu Ma was, in fact, an island. And I'm sure you are thinking, "But that couldn't be. Fortuna Island is supposed to be in Pingu Ma. How can an island be in an island? That just couldn't be." But it can be, and it was. Pingu Ma was a large round island with a large round hole in the middle, and inside that hole was water, and inside that water was another, smaller island. So Fortuna Island is actually an island within an island.

"It's a rare find, it is," Pondro said. "An island within an island. Well, well, what would you be wanting with this Pingu Ma, if you don't mind my asking?"

"I'm planning a fishing expedition. Can I get a copy of this map?"

"Well, well, I suppose that's possible. Why don't you wander up through the book stacks and look for some information on this place while I make you a copy of the map? The geography books are in stack twelve, I believe," said Pondro as he started to gather up the map.

Ridley took one last glance at Pondro's collection of Alaskan maps as he followed him out of the map room. Pedro was waiting to escort him to stack twelve, which gave Ridley the distinct feeling that Pedro had been listening at the door the whole time. And Ridley noticed that he *still* had the spinach stuck in his teeth!

When Ridley left the public library, Pedro, and a once again sleeping Pondro a few hours later, he had a copy of the Pingu Ma map safely tucked in his back pocket and a load of books in his arms.

He always loved this part of a journey – the very beginning. He knew where he was headed, and he couldn't wait to be there. But he didn't know how exactly he would get to Pingu Ma or what he would find when he arrived. He hoped the books would help.

CHAPTER 3

IT WAS IN a book called *The Doughnut-Shaped Island of the South Pacific* that Ridley finally found mention of the flying fish that had gotten him started on this crazy adventure in the first place. The book was a history of the island, its few inhabitants, and the local wildlife. It explained the following:

Legend has it that one species of fish on this island can actually fly. These fish are said to be located in the waters of Fortuna Island itself. However, the existence of these so-called flying fish and the location of their habitat have never been scientifically proven and so remain a mystery to all but the local inhabitants of Pingu Ma.

In another book on South Pacific marine life, *Fish from the South Pacific*, the flying fish were described as follows:

Flying fish usually swim in schools. They average 60 to 140 centimeters in length and have pectoral fins that compare in size with the wings of birds. The pelvic fins are also enlarged. Flying fish generally do not actually fly, but glide on their outstretched fins for distances of up to 250 meters.

But it wasn't until he opened *A Year and a Day in Pingu*

 Pectoral fins: fins on each side of a fish that are behind the head and gills.

Ma that he found a picture of a flying fish.

"Wow!" Ridley exclaimed as he spread open the pages and held up the book. He was dazzled by the sight of the colorful drawing. The flying fish was a huge oval shape with fins extended out like giant wings. The scales on the edge of the fins were rippled, almost feathery in appearance, making the creature look even more as if it were half fish, half bird. The scales were painted silver and gold, making Ridley feel as if he were staring at sunken treasure rather than a picture of a fish.

"Amazing!" Ridley breathed. "Oh yeah, this is going to get me on another magazine cover for sure!" He scanned the rest of the book for more information. It was a memoir written by Sir Jonathan Whimsby, a well-known retired explorer, and quite frankly, a bit of a kook. Apparently, this Whimsby fellow had spent a year and a day living on the island of Pingu Ma some time back, at least twenty years ago. On the back flap of the book, there was a photograph of Sir Jonathan Whimsby. He looked spry and energetic in a khaki safari outfit and a beige canvas jungle hat designed to protect his face from bugs. He was smiling a smile that showed big white teeth, and he was holding up his left hand, on the palm of which sat a hairy tarantula. Beneath the photograph there was a caption that read:

Sir Jonathan Whimsby lives in Wilmington, North-umberland County, England, with three cats and a parakeet named Tootles.

Memoir: a record of personal observations and experiences.

It occurred to Ridley that this Sir Jonathan person would be the best source of information to help prepare him for his expedition to Pingu Ma in search of the flying fish of Fortune Falls. This Whimsby fellow might even be able to explain the box of pink and yellow snoring caterpillars. He was going to have to seek this man out.

Ridley showed his parents the picture of the flying fish and told them all about Sir Jonathan Whimsby. He knew he had to go to England and find this man, but he didn't know how he was going to get there. They all sat down together to draw up a plan.

"I'm sure that Boris would fly him over," Engelbert suggested.

"Who's Boris?" Ridley asked.

"Oh, he's an old friend of your father's," Eugenia explained. "They met down in Brazil a good fifteen years ago, before you were born."

"Boris is our best bet," Engelbert said. "He could probably fly you out in the morning. Eugenia, why don't you take Ridley into the den and make sure he has his traveling papers in order. Give him some pounds sterling as well. I'll call Boris and see what I can set up. We'll have Ridley in England in no time at all!"

Ridley and his mother left his father to arrange the travel plans and got to work packing his gear. It looked as if his fishing expedition was about to begin and that his first stop was destined to be Wilmington, England. That meant

 Pounds sterling: the type of money used in England.

taking allergy medicine because Ridley was desperately allergic to cats.

The Bluefoxes worked late into the night. By the time they were finally all in bed, Ridley's supplies had been sorted, his backpack was organized, and his favorite fishing clothes were clean. When he was traveling, he always wore his fishing hat, sturdy hiking boots (his lucky ones had thick red laces), and khakis.

In the morning, he ate a big breakfast with his mother and father and received their final words of wisdom – "Wash your armpits each day" and "Bugs are a good source of protein" – before they drove him to a small airport located just outside of town. From there, Boris and his plane would take Ridley to England where he would find Sir Jonathan Whimsby.

His father's friend was waiting to help Ridley with his bags when they arrived. Ridley didn't know which made him more nervous, the unlikely character who introduced himself as "Boris Mirsoev, pilot at your service," a happy looking man with a scraggly brown beard and mirrored sunglasses who was standing on the tarmac busily munching on a hamburger, or the so-called plane behind Boris.

Boris continued eating his hamburger with one hand and grabbed Ridley's gear off the ground with the other. He hoisted it onto his shoulder and lumbered toward his aircraft, all the while expelling a series of farts and grunts. Ridley took one look at Boris' ketchup-, mustard-, and relish-covered fingers and decided he didn't want them touching his stuff.

"That's all right," Ridley said as he caught up to Boris and reached for his backpack. "I can carry my own things. You don't have to bother." He put the pack on his own back, waved goodbye to his parents, and walked with Boris toward the aircraft.

Ridley felt a jolt of panic when he got a close look at the "plane" in which they were going to cross the Atlantic Ocean. It was a rickety looking thing that seemed more like a prop on a movie set than an actual apparatus of flight. *The Wright Brothers* *would not approve*, thought Ridley grimly, but he refrained from expressing this thought out loud. The plane was really nothing more than a bucket of rust with a wing and some wheels. It looked as though it were a hundred years old!

The body of the plane had once been painted a bright red but was now faded and covered with rust stains ranging in size from golf ball to tennis ball size. As Ridley climbed through the right side door of the wee plane, he looked up to see Boris stuffing another hamburger into his mouth, lettuce shavings and sauce splattering across his knees. He watched as Boris raised the already half-eaten burger to his lips and shoved it in.

Is this guy going to stop eating long enough to get this sad excuse for a plane off the ground? Ridley thought to himself as he watched Boris chew. Ridley looked away quickly,

---

The Wright Brothers: made the first flight with their flying machine on December 17, 1903.

embarrassed, as he noticed a pickle hanging from the man's scraggly brown beard. It jangled and joggled with each movement of Mirsoev's jaw. *Gross,* thought Ridley, *this guy is really gross.* With a glance toward the rear of the plane, Ridley was dismayed to find that the interior of the little aircraft was pretty gross too. The cargo space was littered with scrunched up wrappers and empty cups. Based on the look of a small puddle of pink crud on the floor, Boris was as fond of strawberry milkshakes as he was of hamburgers.

Boris crammed back another burger and they prepared for the flight. The takeoff was relatively successful, except for an episode that involved an empty milkshake cup that flew up out of the cargo hold and bonked Ridley on the back of the head. And the first few hours of flying went well, even though the nauseating sound of Mirsoev munching on more burgers didn't stop. But then the plane hit turbulence. It was rough going, and Ridley's body bounced about like a rag doll inside the tiny plane. Boris grabbed onto the controls with his greasy hands, which (Ridley was horrified to see) were sliding all over the place as the plane rocked and rolled through the air pockets.

Boris cackled with glee, "I love that Atlantic turbulence! Really makes you feel alive!" The plane flew through another air pocket and the flight smoothed out again. Ridley breathed a sigh of relief and leaned back, releasing his hands from the seatbelt buckle. He'd been holding it in a death grip, knuckles white from tension, as the small plane had been tossed about. As soon as the flight got smoother, Boris began to talk.

"She's a Cessna, you know. Single Engine Aircraft Skyhawk Model 118B. Built in the 1970s, she was. Bought her down at an auction in Wichita. That's in Kansas, where they build them. I painted her myself, once I'd towed her home. Couldn't fly her then, of course – had no propeller. Now they make those McCauley propellers, but this baby's got a genuine Mirsoev propeller. Made it out of the bottom of an old tin boat I found at the dump."

Ridley groaned and slid low in his seat, not wanting to hear any more, but knowing that he would.

"Had to be metal. Was gonna use the wood from an old picnic table bench. But the Cessna's an all-metal plane, so it had to be the boat bottom." Boris continued his monologue of adoration for his plane. "They call it a 'high wing monoplane,' being as it has only one wing across the top instead of two out the sides. Supposed to seat four people, but I usually only take one passenger at a time."

"That's just great. Great. I'm in a plane that is made out of the bottom of a boat. Not just any boat. A boat you found at the dump. That's just *fabulous*!" Ridley burst out. He really couldn't take this. He just wanted to get on the ground.

"It *is* great, isn't it? Ha! That's the spirit! I love to have an enthusiastic passenger with me. Makes for a great flight!" Boris roared in a happy voice. He reached over and slapped Ridley on the back with a grubby hand and grinned at him in pleasure. The rowdy pilot's quick movement suddenly dislodged the pickle that had been dangling in his beard. Ridley was horrified as it was flung out of the crinkly hairs and flew across the cockpit. He screamed as the offensive garnish smacked him in the cheek and stuck to his face. "*Aiieee!*" Ridley yelled and swatted at the pickle until it slid down his cheek and plopped to the floor.

Boris stared at him hard from behind his mirrored sunglasses. Ridley immediately waved his hands around his face and screeched, "*Aiiiiiiiieeeee haaaaa! Woo Hooo!* I love flying!" His effort to cover up the embarrassing pickle predicament paid off. This burst of excitement on Ridley's part brought a smile to the pilot's face and once again, the man began to talk.

Now that Boris was assured of Ridley's enthusiasm (mistakenly, of course), he rattled off all kinds of details about his rust bucket of a plane. Clearly all the talking worked up even more of an appetite. By the time they arrived in England's airspace, Ridley knew the wingspan was eleven meters and that Boris had eaten another two burgers out of the stash he had stowed underneath his seat. Boris gestured so wildly as he talked and ate that most of the ingredients ended up splattered across the instrument panel.

Ridley's face was pinched with nervousness from the flight, but the only change in Boris was a new smudge of mustard on his mirrored sunglasses. What had his father been thinking? This guy was not fit to be a pilot. All Ridley wanted to do now was make it to the ground safely. Ridley prayed that he would survive this last half hour of flight. He stared out the window of the tiny plane and tried to concentrate on what the cover of *Fishin' Fabulous* would look like when he was on it, holding a flying fish from Fortune Falls. It would all be worth it, even this flight with the hamburger eating Boris Mirsoev, once he got his hands on a flying fish.

CHAPTER 4

A QUESTIONABLE LANDING, a hug from the overly expressive pilot that squeezed all of Ridley's breath out, and a two-hour taxi ride later, Ridley stood facing #124 Wyndemire Lane, Wilmington, England. He was nervous and he had need to be if Sir Jonathan Whimsby was anything like his house. It was imposing, to say the least. Sir Whimsby's large home was painted light yellow and had a wide front veranda and many windows. Beautiful dark green ivy was clinging to both sides of the house and growing across the roof. As Ridley started to make his way up the front walkway, he saw that the design of the stained glass windowpane on the door was none other than England's flag, the Union Jack. Ridley held his breath anxiously and pressed the doorbell, which rang out to the tune of "God Save the Queen." Sir Jonathan Whimsby is definitely a man with great patriotism, Ridley thought to himself.

Ridley heard footsteps approaching and then the front door swung slowly inward to reveal a tall, bald man in a black tuxedo. Ridley was so nervous that he didn't even notice that this man looked nothing like the black-and-white picture on the back of *A Year and a Day in Pingu Ma.*

 Veranda: a roofed, open porch on the outside wall of a building.

Ridley began speaking very quickly. "Good day, Sir Whimsby, my name is – " The tall, bald man in the black tuxedo raised his hand in a gesture for silence. "I am Sir Whimsby's butler," the tall, bald man said in a deep, slow voice. "I will see if he is receiving visitors today. Whom shall I say is calling?"

"Oh, um, ah, he, hem …" Ridley cleared his throat. "My name is Ridley Bluefox and I am here to talk to Sir Whimsby about Pingu Ma."

"Very well then, I will see if he has any time for you. Please accompany me to the drawing room where you may rest yourself while you wait," the butler said as he ushered Ridley through a dark, cool entrance hallway and into the adjacent room, closing the door behind him.

The walls in the drawing room were lined in expensive looking bookshelves that held an endless number of leather-bound volumes. There was a fireplace and two antique chesterfields , the kind that have carved wooden lion claws for feet. Ridley sat down and gazed around the room. On the floor in front of him lay a grizzly bearskin rug, its claws and fearsome teeth still intact. Over the fireplace hung the head of a giant wildebeest. Ridley felt as if it were really staring at him with its shiny black eyes.

On the mantel of the fireplace there was a row of picture frames, but instead of photographs, the frames held carefully preserved insects, the likes of which Ridley had never seen before. Only the pins that held each body in

---

Chesterfield: a large couch or sofa, with a back and arms that are the same height.

place reassured him that these exotic bugs were indeed dead. One looked very much like the branch of a tree. Another was a beetle the size of a small child's hand and had a brilliant emerald green shell.

Behind him, the door slammed open and a booming voice rang out. "Pingu Ma! Ah, yes, Pingu Ma! An exotic place – a dangerous place – is Pingu Ma! What is it you want with my precious Pingu Ma?"

Ridley bolted up from his place on the antique chesterfield and turned to meet Sir Jonathan Whimsby.

Sometimes when a man is rather large, he can be described as "a bear of a man," and this was certainly the case for Sir Jonathan Whimsby. Although he may once have been a black bear of a man, he was now, in his old age, a polar bear of a man. Massive in height, with a neck as thick as the thigh of an ordinary person, he had wiry white hair that hung to his shoulders and a full white beard and mustache that hid most of his mouth. His face, beneath all that white hair, looked worn and leathery, and behind round metal spectacles were blue eyes that sparkled with good humor.

Before Ridley could even stammer out a nervous introduction, Sir Whimsby had heaved his large body into an overstuffed chair, thrown his feet up on a worn ottoman ꜱ, and called to his butler, asking for a fire to be built in the hearth ꜱ.

Ridley had found the house imposing from the outside

ꜱ **Ottoman**: a low stool on which to rest your feet or sit.
Hearth: the base and floor of a fireplace, usually made of brick or stone.

and even more intimidating on the inside. Now he was staring at the owner of all the bugs, bearskins, and treasures the yellow house held. This was the man behind the book who was guiding him to Fortune Falls, the man who drew the picture of the flying fish, the man who could tell him exactly how to get to Pingu Ma and get what he wanted.

But for the first time in his twelve years, Ridley didn't know what to say. Finally face-to-face with Sir Jonathan Whimsby, Ridley tried to open his mouth to ask all of his questions, but not one single word came out. He shut his mouth abruptly and his face flushed pink with embarrassment. His mind was absolutely blank!

"I love a good roaring fire, don't you, my boy?" boomed Whimsby. "Come sit down here and tell me what you are doing in my home."

Ridley made his way over to Sir Whimsby and held out his hand. They stared at each other for a moment. Ridley opened his mouth again, but no words were ready to come out. His eyes widened in shame until Sir Whimsby stood up, walked around behind him, and gave Ridley a good smack on the back.

"*Hehemm!* Thank you." Ridley pretended to cough while Sir Whimsby sat back down in his overstuffed chair. Whimsby's whack seemed to knock some courage back into him. He shook his head clear and attempted to speak.

"My name is Ridley Bluefox and I am in search of the flying fish of Fortune Falls. I have come to learn about

Pingu Ma, and I understand that no one knows more about that place than you, sir," he said, managing to introduce himself successfully.

"Well, that last bit would be true," Whimsby mumbled under his breath. "Bluefox, huh? I've heard of you. Saw you on the cover of that fishing magazine some time ago, though in my day you'd have to do a mite more than spear a Pollo Pollo to be a hero of any decent sort." Whimsby snorted at this thought and reached in the direction of a side table from which he took a carved box made of a dark brown, almost black, wood. Sir Whimsby tilted back the lid, took out a leather pouch and a pipe made of the same dark wood as the box.

"This box and pipe were given to me by the villagers on Pingu Ma's outer island," Whimsby began. "They are both made of Bora wood. It is a tall, thick tree that grows on the island of Pingu Ma."

Ridley listened to the old adventurer and watched as his thick fingers reached into the leather pouch and began stuffing his pipe.

"The leaves of the Bora tree are dried by the villagers and smoked," Whimsby explained as he lit his pipe and puffed gently. As he expelled the smoke in a perfectly formed blue-grey smoke ring, a large orange and yellow cat leapt up into Sir Whimsby's lap, and a grey cat climbed onto the ottoman and stretched out at Whimsby's feet.

"The cats like the smell of the Bora leaf smoke,"

Whimsby said as he reached out to stroke the fur of the cat in his lap. "This pipe always lures them out of their hiding spots. This one here is called Marmalade, and that one there," he said, wiggling his toes beneath the cat on the ottoman, "goes by the name of Crumpets. We had a third one, Dandy Boy, and a parakeet named Tootles. They both perished some years ago during an unfortunate incident involving a gang of squirrels out on the front lawn.

Ridley appeared to be listening attentively, but he had no interest in the cats, Tootles, or roving rodents with long bushy tails. Ridley was breathing a sigh of relief because he had remembered to pack his allergy medication. He was also wishing that Whimsby would get on with it already. When was he going to start talking about Pingu Ma?

To turn the subject back to his fishing expedition, Ridley brought out the small cardboard box that looked like Chinese food take-out but really housed the flying fish bait that had started this whole thing in the first place.

"Have you ever seen anything like this?" Ridley asked as he thrust the box in front of Sir Whimsby. "They are supposed to be flying fish bait, specifically for the flying fish of Fortune Falls. They came with a map of The Island of Fortuna."

"Well, let's see what you've got here." Whimsby leaned forward and grabbed the box, peered inside, and said, "What in the Dickens?" Just at that moment, Marmalade stood, stretched, and dug her nails into Sir Whimsby's thigh. With a yelp, Whimsby jumped up out of his chair, upsetting the entire contents of the box that looked like Chinese food take-out. The fuzzy pink and yellow caterpillars flew up out of the box and into the air. Marmalade and Crumpets were ready and waiting as the bait plopped to the carpeted floor.

"Not the bait! Don't let them eat the bait!" Ridley hollered as he dove for the caterpillars, desperate to reach the little creatures before the cats got to them first. The caterpillars were no longer snoring – they were now wide awake, scurrying to and fro at a much faster pace than the average caterpillar is capable of moving. Sir Whimsby was standing on the ottoman laughing in his booming voice, seemingly delighted by the upset. "God bless those cats," he said. "They do keep life interesting."

It was madness and mayhem as Ridley tried to scoop the swift little things up off the floor while Marmalade and Crumpets worked on cornering a couple of them under the chesterfield.

CHAPTER 5

A SHORT WHILE later, the bait had been gathered (one single caterpillar had been lost to Crumpets, who was now curled beneath the couch looking decidedly ill), tea had been served, and everyone had calmed down. Finally, Sir Whimsby began dispensing the advice that Ridley desperately sought.

"Your best way is to go by boat. Yes indeed, boat is the way to go. Get yourself to Thailand. You'll find passage out of Bangkok. Pingu Ma is out past Papua New Guinea and the Soloman Islands. The port is on the west side of the outer island and there lies a small village of a few hundred natives. Go to the marketplace and ask for The Bug Eater. She will be able to identify this caterpillar-creature bait that you have, and she'll probably tell you how to use it, for I confess, I've no idea what those things are. I've never seen such beasts, and I thought I had seen them all!"

"What about the flying fish? How do I catch them?" Ridley asked.

"Oh, I've never seen one of those either." Sir Whimsby shook his head sadly.

"What? But you drew the picture!" Ridley said in surprise. He fumbled around in his backpack and pulled out *A Year and a Day in Pingu Ma.* Pedro and the public library probably wouldn't be too pleased that he'd left the country with the library book, but he was glad he brought it. He flipped through the pages until he found the colorful picture of the flying fish and then held it up for Sir Whimsby to see. "How could you draw this if you haven't seen the flying fish?"

"Oh, my dear boy," Sir Whimsby said, chuckling, and shook his head again. "I didn't draw that picture!"

"But – but – then where did it come from?" Ridley sputtered.

"The picture is of the flying fish, I can assure you that. But I didn't draw it."

"Then how – "

"Stop interrupting and listen up. Maybe you will find out," Sir Whimsby said as he reached over and took the book from Ridley's hands.

"Ah yes," he sighed and began his story. "I received this picture on the same day I ended up leaving Pingu Ma. I hadn't intended to leave, you see, it just worked out that way. I lived on a small but sturdy sea vessel during the course of that year in Pingu Ma. My boat stayed anchored in the harbor and I used it as my home base during the year I explored the islands. I would leave it from time to time and stay for days in the interior, but it was my home most of the time.

"The night I left Pingu Ma was unplanned. It was

storm season, you see, and we'd had many a rough night. But I can handle a little seasickness and my vessel was sturdy, as I said. She was always tightly anchored, so I didn't foresee a problem. I was warned by the locals, of course, that the harbor was not as safe as it seemed, but as I said, I can handle a bitty storm better than most men, so I had no worries. Until Hurricane Bertha showed up, that is. *Whooooeee* she was a wild storm, that one! Tore down trees and capsized boats – must have reduced more than one village to shreds. 'Course, I never saw the full extent of Bertha's damage because she ripped out my anchor and tossed my sea vessel across the ocean like it was nothing more than a badminton birdie! When I woke up the next morning, I was off the coast of Africa. Hah! So there you have it, boy. Hurricane Bertha is the reason I was in Pingu Ma for a year and a day and not a moment longer." Sir Whimsby closed the book and tossed it back to Ridley.

Ridley was staring at him with one eyebrow raised and a look of deep confusion on his face. "What does that have to do with the flying fish?"

"I left unexpectedly boy, didn't you hear me? That is why I didn't get a chance to see the flying fish. I was scheduled to hike into Fortune Falls the next day."

"Oh. But what about the picture?"

"Mmmm, yes. The picture that you see in this book was given to me by a crooked old man that I met on the beach the very day that Hurricane Bertha swept me away,"

Sir Whimsby began.

"Wait a minute! Did you say 'a crooked old man?'" Ridley couldn't believe his ears. Could it possibly be the same crooked old man who had given him the box of bait?

"Yes, that's right. Crooked. Leaned on a walking stick. As I was saying before you interrupted, I was sitting in the marketplace at a juice stand. The crooked old man approached me with that picture and a proposition." Sir Whimsby's eyes took on a faraway look as he recalled that day so long ago.

"'Are you the adventurer Whimsby?' the crooked old man asked me in a gravelly voice.

"'Yes,' I answered. I was not surprised to be sought out. I'd made quite a name for myself with the locals.

"'You like to catch things, don't you, Whimsby? You like to catch creatures and pin them into boxes and keep them, don't you?'

"'Why, yes, I do!' I answered the crooked old man. 'I have caught many fine specimens in the jungles here,' I told him. He squinted his eyes at me and slid that picture across the table.

"'I'll bet you've never seen anything like this,' he said in a low voice. And then he told me about the flying fish of Fortune Falls. Now, it is true that I had never seen a flying fish like the one in the picture he gave me that day. I have, however, heard of them before. I had an old friend back in college, Ronald was his name, a fishing man, much like yourself. He was always going on about these flying fish. Researching and reading, trying to locate them, you know?"

"Well, did he?" Ridley interrupted.

"Hm? Did he what?"

"Did he locate the flying fish? Did he catch one?" Ridley said in a panicky voice. How could Sir Whimsby not see how important this was? After all, there would be no point to this journey if some other fisherman had done it all before.

"No, no. Not that anyone is aware of anyway. This chap ended up quitting college. Said he'd found new information on the whereabouts of the flying fish and off he went. No one ever heard from him again. It was as if he just disappeared off the face of the planet." Sir Whimsby was quiet for a moment while he reflected on the fate of his school friend. "Anyway, the crooked old man on the island said that these flying fish couldn't be found anywhere else in the world. Imagine that! Ronald drove himself crazy searching for these fish and here I had stumbled onto them by accident! So when the crooked old man offered to meet me at the juice hut again the next day, I said I would definitely be there! He said he would give me some bait that would ensure a fine catch and a map that would take me right to the site of the flying fish. Naturally the picture aroused my adventurer's instinct and I wanted to add one of the magnificent flying fish to my collection of stuffed and mounted Pingu Ma specimens. Everything was set for the next day. If it wasn't for Hurricane Bertha, there would be a stuffed and mounted flying fish in this room right now, I can assure you of that!" As if to prove his point, Sir Whimsby gestured around the room with his hands.

"I see. But you didn't catch one," Ridley pointed out.

"Only because of the hurricane," Sir Whimsby reassured.

"Oh, of course, only because of the hurricane," Ridley repeated. His mind was moving a mile a minute. No hurricane was going to get in his way. He was going to be the first to bring home a flying fish. This catch was going to make him more famous than ever. Then he thought about the crooked man. Was it even possible that it was the same crooked man he had met? Sir Whimsby's story must be at least twenty years old. Could the same man show up in Northern Ontario twenty years later?

"What did the bait look like?" Ridley asked "Didn't it look like this?" He shook the box of caterpillars.

"But, my boy, I have told you this already. I've never seen anything like that box you have there. The crooked old man mentioned the bait but said he would give it to me the next day. Then Hurricane – "

"I know, I remember. Hurricane Bertha," Ridley sighed.

"Tell you what – find a woman called The Bug Eater. She will make sure you know what those creatures are and what you need to do to catch these fish you are after."

Ridley pulled a small spiral-bound pad of paper out of his backpack and scribbled down some notes. Now that he was actually getting some of the information he had come for, he didn't want to forget a thing.

"What's her name? This woman I should find?" Ridley asked.

"You need to listen better, boy," said Sir Whimsby, so Ridley wrote down "The Bug Eater" with a big question mark on his notepad and let Sir Whimsby finish.

"Now, Pingu Ma is small, but it is still an easy place in which to get oneself utterly and hopelessly lost. So you mind what The Bug Eater tells you." Whimsby stopped talking for a moment and stared off into space as he decided what else was necessary information for Ridley, and what the boy would just have to learn on his own. "While you are there, sleep with your shoes on. The spiders are as big as dinner plates and like to bite. Just trust me on that one, my boy."

"Look, I'm not some little boy!" Ridley insisted. He didn't like the idea that this strong, adventurous man thought of him as just some kid.

"Sure you are," Sir Whimsby said as he laughed and looked Ridley up and down. "What are you, ten? But good for you, showing up at my home like this. That takes some guts, that does."

Ridley was appalled that Sir Whimsby thought he was ten. How embarrassing! But before he could correct him, he was being ushered out of the imposing yellow house. His visit was over, apparently.

Both Sir Jonathan Whimsby and his bald butler walked Ridley to the front door. Sir Whimsby smiled, showing off his huge white teeth, and shook Ridley's hand, wishing him the best of luck. As Ridley walked down the path toward the road, he heard Sir Whimsby mutter, "There goes a crazy fool."

* * *

From the home of Sir Jonathan Whimsby, Ridley taxied back to the airport and took a flight out of England, bound for Moscow.

From Moscow he flew to Tehran.

From Tehran, he flew to Calcutta where he boarded a train bound for Dhaka.

In Dhaka, he boarded another plane, this one bound for Bangkok.

From Bangkok, he got on a boat headed for Port Morsby in Papua New Guinea.

Here he located a captain of yet another boat to take him out past Soloman Islands to Pingu Ma.

CHAPTER 6

FOR A WHILE Ridley mulled over Sir Whimsby's comment that he was a "crazy fool." In fact, he mulled it over in his mind during his whole trip to the shores of Pingu Ma and especially at each stop along the way, of which there were many. By the time he finally reached the port located on the west side of the outer island, Ridley was beginning to understand that he was in fact a "crazy fool" for ever undertaking this fishing expedition. And it was all to catch some flying fish that half of the world had never even heard of. Fish that he was after only because a crooked old man in Northern Ontario said he couldn't catch them. *Bah*, he thought. *I will catch them. After all I've gone through so far, I had better!*

It was very early in the morning when Ridley finally arrived in Pingu Ma. Even from the boat, Ridley could tell that the island was the most luscious looking place that he had ever set eyes upon. And you must remember that Ridley had been traveling the world over ever since he had been a baby Bluefox. His parents had forced him to tag along on many journeys to far-off, exotic locales. He had seen a lot of different places and was relatively hard to impress.

Perhaps it was how much he had gone through to get

to the shores of this island. Or maybe it was the way the fog rising off the ocean gave the island a mysterious quality. Whatever the reason, Pingu Ma was a stunning sight to behold. Everything Ridley could see was a lush, vibrant green. The vegetation was thick and tropical, and a pristine white sand beach sat in a ring around the emerald greenness, separating it from the clear blue ocean. It was breathtaking. Ridley immediately understood why Sir Jonathan Whimsby was so fond of this place.

There were villagers walking up and down the beach on their way to and from a small marketplace at the port. Ridley joined those who were walking toward the market. They smiled and returned his friendly greetings, until, that is, he asked about The Bug Eater. As soon as those three words came out of Ridley's mouth, the villagers would turn away from him. Five times he tried to ask someone about The Bug Eater. Each time he got the same response. The villager would look at him, horrified by the question, and then abruptly turn and walk away. Once the rest of the people on the beach realized what he was asking, they ignored him completely, no longer even bothering with a greeting or a nod hello. After several minutes of this, a young girl around the age of seven or eight, walked right up to Ridley and peered at him with interest.

She was all skinny arms and boney knees sticking out of a plain cotton jumper. She had tangled black hair that she had to keep pushing back out of her face. Staring at him with her big brown eyes, she said, "They won't tell you where to find The Bug Eater because they think she is wicked. But I will take you to her. She has a hut at the end of the marketplace. She is always sitting in there, waiting. Today she will be waiting for you!" she said as she skipped ahead and motioned for Ridley to follow.

"How on earth could this little girl help me?" Ridley muttered to himself. "I'm certainly not going to start following her around. I mean really, I am Ridley Bluefox. Besides, how on earth can The Bug Eater be waiting for me when no one even knows I'm here? And what does she mean, 'wicked?' What, like a witch or something? Maybe Sir Whimsby is playing a trick on me. He probably doesn't want me to catch a flying fish. He probably thinks I'll look better than him when I do. Well, too bad for him. I can handle some weird bug lady, no problem."

While Ridley was talking to himself, the young girl had continued to skip toward the marketplace. She stopped when she realized that Ridley wasn't following along behind her. She waved her skinny arms above her head and shouted out, "Come on then! No one else here will show you where she is!"

"All right, all right," he said under his breath. He jogged to catch up to his new guide.

They walked past melon stands and a fish seller, bins of fruit, nuts, and even a small tea hut that sold cold refreshments to the local shoppers. People were milling from stand to stand, filling their baskets with food and supplies. Ridley noticed that people seemed to step away from the young girl he was following. The fruit sellers would call out their prices to the others, but none of them would call out to her.

This continued as she lead him through the market-place. The hut they were headed for was set a short distance from the last fruit stand. There were no people near this hut at all, but there seemed to be a lot more flies here than anywhere else.

The Bug Eater's hut was made of mud and dried grass, and the first thing that Ridley noticed was the odd smell that was wafting out of a hole cut into its wall. The young girl pointed at the doorway, which only came up to Ridley's waist, and said, "You must crawl through here to see The Bug Eater."

"Shouldn't I knock or announce myself?" Ridley asked. "I can't just crawl through there!"

"She knows that you are coming. She is waiting. She knows everything because of the bugs," the young guide explained as she pushed Ridley closer to the hole in the mud hut. He crouched low to the ground and crawled on all fours through the hole in the mud hut that served as a doorway.

Ridley paused briefly and glanced back at the market-place. He saw that many of the villagers had stopped going about their business and stood still, looking, watching to see what would happen. This unexpected audience made Ridley nervous, but he had come this far, so he must continue.

CHAPTER 7

AS RIDLEY MOVED farther into the hut and breathed in the rancid air, he recalled Sir Whimsby's words again: "There goes a crazy fool."

Once deep inside, Ridley sat against the inner wall and let his eyes become accustomed to the darkness. The Bug Eater's dwelling was dim, stinky, and hazy with smoke. He recognized it as the same smoke smell that had come from Sir Whimsby's pipe. But underneath the smoke smell, there was that odor that he'd first noticed outside the hut. It was much stronger inside, filling up his nostrils so that he could almost taste it.

"Ugh," Ridley breathed out and covered his mouth and nose with his sleeve. "What *is* that?" He looked around, trying to locate the origin of the stench.

There it was. It was her. In the center of the room burned a small fire and behind it sat a tiny woman. She was sitting cross-legged on the ground, smoking a wooden pipe.

Ridley leaned closer to the fire and looked into the face of the tiny woman. She smiled a wide grin that revealed rotten teeth clamped down on the stem of her pipe. She had long, dirty hair that hung to the ground and she was wrapped in a dress that was no more than a rag. She had

Rancid: having a disgusting smell or taste, like that of decomposing fats or oils.

dark stains on her fingers and the odor emanating from her was so strong that it made Ridley's eyes water.

"You have come for the *feeeessssshhhh*," The Bug Eater whispered. "You have come for the feeessshh that no one has ever caught." She paused before hissing, "*Bluuuuuuuuffffooooooxxxxxx*."

Ridley was shocked. The young girl had been right. He took out the cardboard box that looked like Chinese food take-out and held it toward the tiny woman. "What are these?" he asked.

She waved the box away, apparently not having to look in order to know what was inside. "The crooked man who sold you the bait was wrong," she whispered across the fire. "He did not know what he thought he knew. They are not bait for the flying fish, but a defense against the beast that protects the fish you seek."

"Hold on," Ridley interrupted. "What kind of beast are we talking about here?"

"The kind of beast that is impossible to pass without those creatures," The Bug Eater said as she pointed at the box. She whispered, "You will need those on your journey, or you will not get to where you want to go." Ridley couldn't help but wish that she'd be a little more specific. Listening to The Bug Eater felt like putting a puzzle together without the box top to help him figure out what picture he was supposed to be making with all the pieces. It was confusing, to say the least.

"How do you know these things?" Ridley asked the tiny woman.

"The bugs help me to see. You will see too. You will eat and you will see." She reached behind her back and presented a basket woven out of grass. The stench hit him square in the face. The basket was full of what Ridley realized must be dung. It was dark, steaming, and odorous. No wonder the hut had such a stink to it! The tiny lady reached inside the basket of dung and pulled out a fluorescent yellow beetle. She brought her hand to her mouth and snapped the beetle in half between her rotten teeth before shoving the whole thing in her mouth. Beetle juice ran down her chin and fingers.

"You will eat. You will sleep. Then you will know," she whispered. Ridley's eyes widened in horror. He shook his head and leaned away as he watched her reach once more into the basket of dung, pull out a beetle, and snap the bug body in half. Popping one half into her mouth, she rose to her knees, passed the dripping remainder across the fire to Ridley, and pressed it against his lips. He ate.

CHAPTER 8

RIDLEY CLOSED HIS eyes as he chewed and swallowed the awful thing. Immediately he became drowsy. He lay down beside the fire and curled up into a ball. Within minutes he was asleep. The easiest way to explain what happened next would be to say that he had a dream. In his dream, there was a bit of his past, a bit of his present, and a bit of his future.

He found himself in a dense jungle, surrounded by Bora trees. Looking up, he saw Sir Whimsby and the bald butler perched in the crook of a tree branch. They were holding Marmalade and Crumpets. Instinctively, Ridley reached into his pocket for his allergy medication. But then he realized that he was dreaming and he couldn't be allergic to cats in a dream, could he?

"Hang on a minute," Ridley said to himself. "What kind of dream am I having if I know that I'm dreaming? And if I can talk to myself?" He turned his attention back to the cats as Crumpets hacked up the pink and yellow caterpillar. The insect fell out of the tree and down to the ground where it bounced at Ridley's feet. Ridley bent to pick it up and put it in the pocket of his trousers. Sir Whimsby called his name and said, "You will get lost unless you bring the girl along." At that moment, the young village girl stepped out from behind one of the Bora trees. She smiled at him and said, "I am Mayuri. I will show you the way to Fortuna Island."

As the dream continued, Mayuri lead Ridley through the jungle to the edge of a crystal clear pond. Ridley scanned his surroundings. He could see smooth shapes moving in the depths of the pond.

Up out of the water flew great flying fish. They were gigantic and had scales that glittered silver and gold. The fish dove back down into the water and swam to a waterfall across the pond. In his dream, Ridley and Mayuri glided across the water. As they approached the waterfall, it parted in two, like a curtain made of water. He could see an archway carved into the rock. Through it swam schools of flying fish. Now and then, one would emerge up out of the water, fly a few meters, and then dive back down. Ridley wanted to pass through the arch and follow the beautiful fish into the grotto, but the curtains of water folded back on themselves, and out of the base of the waterfall rose a witch. She shrieked at them in a deafening, high-pitched voice. Ridley watched Mayuri clamp her hands over her ears in an effort to block out the painful noise. The giant water witch threw her head back and shrieked again. Her body shook as she continued to make the awful, brain-numbing sound.

Ridley awoke from the dream with a start. He was shivering and shaking, even though he was still curled up by the fire in The Bug Eater's hut. She was staring at him from across the room – grinning at him with her rotten teeth. The basket of yellow fluorescent beetles and dung was stowed away from view, and The Bug Eater was once again smoking the Bora pipe.

"What did you do to me?" he coughed out. She laughed a dry laugh and said, "The bugs told you, didn't they? They always tell you what you want to know."

Ridley stared at the offensive woman and buried his face in his palms. "'Wicked' is right!" he muttered.

Ridley got up onto his hands and knees and crawled out the doorway, dragging his backpack behind him. Once outside, he leaned up against the side of the hut, put his head between his knees, took great gulps of the fresh air and threw up twice. A little while later, the village girl approached Ridley and put her small hand in his. Ridley was so shaken by his creepy experience in the hut that he didn't even think twice about getting help from a little girl.

He let her lead him back through the marketplace and down the beach to the water's edge. When they got there, she sat on the sand and waited while Ridley washed his mouth and his face with seawater. He scrubbed himself furiously with the salty water, ignoring how it stung his eyes, wanting only to rinse away the taste of his time with The Bug Eater.

Resting on the beach, his mind revisited all that had happened in the dream he'd had in the awful hut. As if to test if the whole experience were real, he slipped his hand into his pocket. His eyes widened in disbelief and he pulled out the pink and yellow caterpillar that had been previously lost to Crumpets the cat. As a further test, he turned to the young village girl and asked, "Are you called Mayuri?" The young village girl nodded her head and her mouth spread into a happy smile. "I am Mayuri," she responded in a soft voice. "I think you now understand why the others say that The Bug Eater is wicked."

"Yeah, I guess so," Ridley said as he sighed and lay back on the beach. Mayuri sat down beside him in the sand. They stayed that way for a bit, just listening to the waves lapping at the shore. Once Ridley had recuperated, he sat up and turned to Mayuri.

"How come everyone else is so afraid of The Bug Eater but you are not?" Ridley asked. Mayuri looked down at her toes and dug them into the sand. Her cheeks flushed in embarrassment. Ridley pressed the question. "You said that everyone here thinks she is wicked. That's why they ignored me when I was asking for directions. Only you would help me. How come they are afraid and you are not? And why did they all move away from you when we were in the market? You're just a little girl!"

Mayuri looked at Ridley and whispered, "She's my mother."

"What? That's your mom?" Ridley blurted out in shock. Mayuri looked back down at the sand, and her cheeks flushed an even deeper shade. Ridley realized that he had embarrassed her. He felt badly about it, but more than that, he was uncomfortable with her silence. He changed the topic and began to recount his dream to his new young friend. He even showed her the pink and yellow caterpillar that had somehow traveled back through the dream with him.

"How do you know that these flying fish are actually there?" Mayuri asked. Ridley dug out the map he got from the public library and handed it to Mayuri. He also showed her the poem from the cardboard box of caterpillars. Mayuri took a close look at the old map and then read through the poem a couple of times before she said, "But this says the flying fish cannot be caught!"

"Well yeah, but I'm not just anybody, so that doesn't really count for me," Ridley explained. "You may not know this, but I'm a famous fisherman. You're actually pretty lucky to get to hang out with me. I've been on magazine covers and everything," Ridley boasted. He was starting to feel more like himself again.

"What's a magazine?" Mayuri asked him.

"What's a magazine? Are you serious? Oh, never mind!" Ridley dismissed the comment with a wave of his hand. "Just trust me, I'm famous. Now listen, here's what we're going to do. You're going to take me across the outer island of Pingu Ma and the interior waters to Fortuna Island." Ridley spread his map on the ground and showed her where he wanted to go.

"We'll take the most direct route through here," he said as he dragged his finger across the map, "because I don't want to waste any more time. I need to get to these fish."

"But this is a dangerous path you have chosen. If we went the long way across, like this," Mayuri said as she drew an alternate path onto the map, "then it would be a safer journey."

"No, I don't have time for that. Besides, I can handle a little danger. I'm Ridley Bluefox. I do this all the time. Now listen, once we get to Fortune Falls, you will follow me into the grotto, but then you can't touch anything. I fish alone," he announced in a stern and serious voice.

"I will guide you through the jungle to the falls …" Mayuri began.

"'Guide' really isn't the right word," Ridley interrupted. "It's more like you are coming along with me, see?"

Mayuri looked at him quizzically for a moment before continuing. "I will go along with you through the jungle to the falls, but I will not cross the archway into the grotto. The grotto is a sacred place. The inhabitants of our island do not go there, because no one ever comes back out," she explained.

"What? Why not? That's ridiculous."

"Some people would say that you should not go there either," she suggested.

"Excuse me? As if! I'll be in and out of there in no time. No one will even know that I was there. And then I'll be on my way home with my prize catch. I'll be on the cover of

Fishin' Fabulous and everyone will be amazed because once again, Ridley Bluefox caught something no one else could catch! Now are you coming or what?" he demanded. His eyes were sparkling with the excitement of being so close to the flying fish, and he was ready to move out onto the final leg of this journey.

Mayuri nodded her head and helped him fold up the map while he reviewed the supplies in his backpack and placed the caterpillar from his trouser pocket back in the cardboard box that looked like Chinese food take-out. Then the unlikely pair set off back through the marketplace, past The Bug Eater's hut (just looking at it made Ridley shudder in disgust), and up the path.

"Now remember, I'll take you there, but I am not going inside the grotto," Mayuri reminded Ridley.

"I know, I know, it's sacred or something, whatever!" Ridley reassured her. "I don't need you in there anyway, you'll just get in the way of my fishing. So don't worry about it. Let's just get moving. The sooner we get to the sacred grotto, the sooner you don't have to go in." And with those words, he sped up his walking pace and headed into the interior of the island.

CHAPTER 9

THE SUN WAS beating down on their backs. The ground was dusty beneath their feet. Every so often, Ridley and Mayuri walked through a small village. Each one was a circle of mud huts around an open area with a large fire pit. Villagers stood in the doorways watching silently as Ridley and Mayuri walked by.

"Why do they all just stand and stare like that?" Ridley asked. He secretly hoped that these people knew who he was and were awed to see a famous fisherman.

Mayuri burst his bubble when she explained, "They all know who my mother is. They think I must be wicked too because I am her child." She was silent for a moment before adding, "But I'm not, you know. I'm not wicked. And I'm not all that little either." She glared at Ridley when she made this last remark.

By early afternoon, they had passed the last of these mud huts behind. Mayuri seemed much more comfortable once they had left the watchful eyes of the villagers. Ridley was pleased that she could manage to keep up with his fast pace. He didn't want her slowing him down.

For hours, they walked through fields of tall grass that scratched at their legs, until eventually they came to the edge of a jungle. Here Mayuri reached a hand out to Ridley to stop him from entering the forest.

"Are you sure you want to continue this way? We can go around this jungle. It may take a little longer, but it will be safer," she said.

"Why would I want to do that?" Ridley asked in disbelief. "Don't be ridiculous. We don't have any time to loose. The sooner I can get to Fortune Falls and back, the better, remember?" he said as he pushed her hand away and entered the jungle. "Besides, how dangerous can it be? All I see is a bunch of trees." Ridley looked around. The trees did look vaguely familiar to him, like the ones in his dream. They had thick trunks and low hanging branches, perfect for climbing. The leaves were a dark velvety green and the size of the palm of a large man's hand – round at the stem, extending into a perfectly pointed tip.

"They're Bora trees," Mayuri said. "The islanders do not allow visitors into the Bora forest. The leaves are – "

"I know, I know," Ridley interrupted. "The leaves are smoked and the villagers of Pingu Ma carve the wood." He finished her explanation while picturing in his mind Sir Whimsby's wooden box and pipe. He stopped walking in order to stare up into one of the trees. Mayuri stood beside him, glancing around from side to side.

"This forest is very well protected," she whispered nervously.

"Yeah right. No one even saw us come in! In fact, we

haven't passed anyone at all since we walked through that last village." Ridley brushed off her warning and started walking again.

They continued this way for a while, with Ridley scoffing at Mayuri's concern as she looked back over her shoulder every few steps, when suddenly they heard a grunt: "*Hunghf!*"

"*Hunghf!*" they heard again. Ridley came to an abrupt halt and turned on Mayuri.

"Was that you?" he narrowed his eyes suspiciously.

"No!" she squeaked in a small voice, her brown eyes wide.

"*Hunghf HUNGHF!*" There it was again!

"Mayuri," Ridley spoke her name slowly while he turned in a circle, peering through the trees. "What exactly is it that protects these trees?"

"Boars. They filled the jungle with boars. Really hungry, angry boars," she answered. "I told you there was a safer way to go."

"Boars? You mean like pigs? That's all we're worried about here? Ha!" Ridley laughed. "I was actually worried for a minute and – "

He was interrupted by scuffling and the snapping of twigs as something began to charge through the trees right toward them.

"*HUUUUNNNNGGUUUUUNGGGGHHHHFFFFFF!*" A wild boar burst through the trees to the left of them.

"That's not a pig!" Ridley yelled. He was staring at an awful beast. It was the size of a large pig but grey and black in color with coarse hairs sprouting out all over it. It had beady yellow eyes and two huge tusks that were so pointed, it was possible someone had sharpened them on purpose. The beast ripped up the ground with its front hooves and snorted air through its snout as it ran.

"That is not a pig!" Ridley shouted again and took off. He was running as fast as his legs could carry him, and Mayuri was right beside him puffing her cheeks out and pumping her arms in effort.

"That! Is! Not! A! Pig!" he yelled between breaths.

"I said 'boar!'" she hollered back as she sped up and ran in front of him. "And there are more!"

"More?" Ridley glanced back over his shoulder. Sure enough, two additional ugly beasts had joined the chase. They were galloping at what felt like breakneck speed and gaining on them every second.

"What? Do? We? Do?" he cried between gasping breaths.

"Keep running!" she answered, and the chase continued. They bashed their way through the Bora trees. Mayuri lead the way. Ridley rationalized that this was because she was not carrying a backpack. Otherwise, she could never have run so fast.

Over roots and under branches they charged. The end of the jungle was only minutes away, though the minutes passed slowly as Ridley ran and ran, ignoring the burning in his lungs and the cramp in his side. Bursting through the last row of trees, they skidded to a halt. They were at the top of a cliff with nowhere to go. Glancing over his shoulder again, Ridley could see that the wild boars were not going to give up the chase at the jungle's end. The beastly things were barreling past the last trees and were now headed right for them, cliff or no cliff.

"Now what?" he panted, looking desperately for an escape. Mayuri turned to him. Her chest was heaving from the effort of running. She shrugged her shoulders and said, "We go down." And then she disappeared.

"Wait!" Ridley called, but it was too late. She'd stepped over the edge. He looked over the cliff to see Mayuri tumbling down the sandy slope. It was the cliff or the boars, and he wasn't about to be something's lunch.

Ridley stepped over the edge of the cliff onto the sandy slope. He managed to keep his footing and slid the first few meters on two feet. Then he hit a root that was sticking out of the sand, and he flew into a tumble. Head over heels and hand over foot, he somersaulted down the sandy slope until he crashed onto the beach at the bottom. Gingerly, he untangled his arms and legs, checking his extremities. It was hard to believe, but nothing was broken. He unhooked his backpack and quickly sorted through his gear.

"Amazing! Nothing's broken in here either," he said as he rummaged through his bag. Ridley turned to Mayuri to see how she'd managed the tumble. She was standing on the beach at the water's edge, brushing herself off and shaking sand out of her hair. She gave him a smile. "We're here."

They'd crossed the outer, doughnut-shaped island and the Bora jungle. The cliff fall had brought them to the inner shore. From where they stood, they could see the form of Fortuna Island in the distance.

Ridley took one last look up the cliff. "I guess we could take the long way when we go home. I mean, if you want to," he said to Mayuri as they headed down the beach.

Mayuri led Ridley south along the shoreline until they came upon a raft that floated in shallow water and was tied to a tough, sandy bush.

"We will use this to cross the water," said Mayuri as she untied the rope that anchored the raft. Ridley glanced from Mayuri to the raft and back to Mayuri, before he voiced his concern. "That raft doesn't look very safe to me."

"Don't be afraid. It is used all the time," Mayuri explained. "The waters between here and Fortuna Island are shallow. They would only come up to your waist. We could walk right through the water over to the island if it weren't for the eels. So we will take the raft."

"I didn't say I was afraid. As if I would be afraid! I was just saying it doesn't look all that safe. But I don't mind." Ridley spoke quickly as they pushed the raft out.

Mayuri used a long pole to move them through the water. She stood at the front of the raft, reaching in with the pole until it struck the sandy bottom, and then she pulled the raft forward with all of her strength. Soon they were well on their way toward Fortuna Island.

"I can do that, you know," Ridley said. "If I did it we'd get there faster. Obviously I'm a lot stronger than you are." Mayuri gave him a strange look and handed over the pole.

As Ridley moved the raft closer to the shore, he understood why Mayuri had warned him about the eels. The waist-deep water that he was poling the raft through was frothing and roiling with the long grey bodies. The closer they got to the island, the more the water seemed as if it was filled with a tangle of snakes. He leaned over to get a closer look when an eel's head poked out of the tangle and snapped its jaws at Ridley's face. Mayuri grabbed onto his shirt and yanked him back just in time.

"Careful not to get too close!" she warned him. "They'll bite!"

"Yeah, I noticed!" Ridley said as he ran his hands over his face and made sure his nose was still where it belonged. He glanced around the raft only to find that they were surrounded by eels on all sides. He looked up at the island, which seemed a lot farther away now that they were balancing on water crammed full of ferocious eels. Ridley could see that it was going to take a bit of work to get them safely across.

Roiling: to be in turbulence or agitation.

CHAPTER 10

RIDLEY AND MAYURI stood on opposite ends of the raft, trying to balance it out as the eel-infested water rolled beneath them.

"How are we going to do this?" Ridley hollered.

"Very carefully?" Mayuri suggested.

"All right, listen. I'll pole us through the eels, but you have to keep an eye out and tell me which direction to go in," Ridley instructed. He wiped the sweat off his brow with the back of his hand and steadied himself for the task ahead. He had to place the long pole into the water very carefully. He shoved it down into the water only to pierce one of the eels. It was impossible to get around them. Each time an eel was hit, it would rear its head out of the tangled mass, gnashing razor-sharp teeth. Ridley wasn't as worried about the eels getting hurt as he was that one of them would upset the raft and he and Mayuri would tumble into the water. So Ridley and Mayuri worked very carefully to move the raft across the water, inching it closer to the shore.

A few hours later, the light was getting dim and the raft finally hit the beach of Fortuna Island. Here the water was too shallow for the eels, so he and Mayuri could safely disembark and drag the raft up onto the beach so that it would not float away. They would need it for the return trip.

The beach on Fortuna Island was a narrow strip of land much rockier than the white sands of Pingu Ma and led right into the jungle. After tying the raft and long pole to a tree on the edge of the beach, Ridley shouldered his backpack of supplies and followed Mayuri into the jungle.

It was humid inside the dense foliage , and Ridley continued to sweat. They were following a path through vegetation so thick that Mayuri and Ridley had to constantly push dangling vines, large tropical leaves, and branches out of their way. They also had to look out for roots growing up out of the ground. This was not the best place to trip and sprain an ankle.

After an hour or so of pushing their way through the jungle, they were ready to stop and set up camp for the night. In the twilight, it would no longer be safe to continue traveling. As it became dark, their surroundings took on an ominous mood, which gave Ridley shivers up and down his spine. He realized that camping here meant spending the night with jungle creatures. He shuddered as he recalled Sir Whimsby's warning about spiders the size of dinner plates.

He and Mayuri made a small clearing in the underbrush, large enough for them to create a fire pit and room to sleep. Ridley hoped that the glowing embers of a small fire would keep any dangerous predators away. Once they had the fire going, Ridley took out the last of his food supply. He helped himself to a fistful of dried fruit and trail

Foliage: a cluster of leaves, flowers, or branches on plants or trees.

mix before passing the rest to Mayuri. She accepted the snack with a nod of thanks and sniffed at it a bit before placing a few pieces in her mouth. Once she decided it was acceptable fare, she shoved the rest in her mouth and chewed heartily.

After they had eaten, Mayuri sat down beside Ridley with a bundle of vines and large leaves that she had set aside when they'd cleared a spot for the fire on the jungle floor. She explained to Ridley, "You will be safe in your shoes, but I have to wrap my bare feet in banana leaves to protect them from the jungle spiders. We will use these vines to tie down your trousers at the ankles. That way, nothing will crawl up your pant legs."

"What about the rest of my body?" asked Ridley, trying to hide the concern in his voice.

"Don't be afraid," Mayuri tried to reassure him with a smile. "We will be safe beside the fire. If we lay with our heads close to the light, then only our legs will be in the darkness. The spiders are afraid of the flames," Mayuri explained in a calm and confident voice.

"I'm not afraid," Ridley said through clenched teeth. But for someone who wasn't afraid, it took Ridley an awfully long time to fall asleep. He kept thinking he felt spiders on his legs. He tried to distract himself by imagining what the next day had in store for him. Would there really be a water witch? Nothing could be as horrific as the witch in his dream, right? But never mind. Water witch or no water witch, he was getting his hands on that fish and his face on a magazine!

Mayuri had none of these concerns. She seemed used to the jungle spiders, so she was asleep in minutes, her soft breathing a comforting reminder to Ridley that he was not alone.

*   *   *

Ridley awoke slowly with the dawn, and his body felt stiff and cold from sleeping on the ground. He turned his head to see if the fire was still going and saw that his left hand had grown all kinds of coarse black hair overnight. He blinked his eyes and wondered how that had happened. One of his eight hairy fingers moved, and he let out a yell as he realized that the black coarse hairs belonged to a gargantuan jungle spider that was sitting on top of his hand. It was mammoth in size, its legs like hairy hotdogs sticking out of a plump, round body that looked like a Valencia orange only black.

"Get-it-off-get-it-off-get-it-off!" yelled Ridley as he jumped up and danced around the clearing in a panic. The spider fell off immediately and scuttled away into the lush jungle foliage that was all around him. Mayuri, who had been sitting up waiting for Ridley to awaken, burst out in peals of laughter. She jumped up too and danced around, mimicking Ridley. "Get-it-off-get-it-off-get-it-off!" and

---

Valencia orange: a type of orange that is very sweet and has few seeds and a thin skin.
Mimic: to imitate; to act or speak like someone in an attempt to make fun of them.

collapsed on the ground in a fit of laughter.

"It's not funny!" hollered Ridley. His temper had gotten the best of him. "I thought you said they were afraid of the fire!"

"They are afraid of the fire," responded Mayuri between fits of giggles. "But as you can see, our fire burned out while we were sleeping! Come on, at least it didn't bite you."

Ridley grumbled to himself as he picked up his backpack and prepared to leave. This little girl was brave while he was acting like a scaredy cat. He was tougher than that! After all, he was Ridley Bluefox. He'd been on fourteen magazine covers for catching exotic (and even dangerous) fish from all over the world. These thoughts renewed his courage and energy, and with that the adventurer and his young guide re-entered the dense jungle and pushed forward to Fortune Falls.

They reached the falls around noon or so, Ridley figured, because the sun was positioned high up in the center of the sky. Coming out of the humid jungle was a relief, but Ridley started to shuffle his feet back and forth when he saw the waterfall. He rubbed his hands together and cracked his knuckles nervously. Fortune Falls was huge! It ran down a cliff that was as tall as a ten-story building. The water pooled at the base of the falls and then ran off into a small river heading for the depths of the jungle. He could see that the best approach would be to walk around the pool of water toward the rock face of the cliff. He got out the cardboard box and held it in his hands. He and Mayuri walked together until they reached the rocks.

"I can't go any farther with you. You will have to make the rest of this trip on your own," Mayuri reminded him and explained that she would wait for him at the edge of the water pool.

Ridley nodded in understanding and climbed up onto the rocks. He carefully made his way along the cliff wall toward the falls. Cracking his knuckles again, he shook out his arms and prepared to face whatever was coming at him next.

CHAPTER 11

RIDLEY NEEDED TO get through the waterfall and into the grotto. He had to catch this fish. Otherwise, the crooked old man at the bait shop would be right. Otherwise, Sir Whimsby would decide Ridley really was a fool. Otherwise, he'd have to go home empty-handed, and that was not going to happen.

"One of these flying fish is mine!" he whispered and clenched his fists in determination as he took another step forward.

Ridley had just glimpsed behind the falls to see that there was indeed an arch and passage cut into the rock, when water sprayed up out of the pool in every direction. Out of the frothing water at the base of falls rose the water witch from his dream! He pressed back against the rocks and prayed that he would not slip and fall into the water.

The creature rose up on a wave in front of him. Her skin was covered in smooth green and blue scales that were the color of jewels. She had a long body and fins like a fish, but her head was like that of a human. There were three slits in each cheek that looked like fish gills. Instead of hair, her head was covered in long, slimy strands of seaweed that hung down her back.

The water witch opened her mouth and let out an earth-shattering shriek. Her lips curled back to reveal a double row of teeth that were jagged like shattered glass. It reminded Ridley of the mouth of a huge barracuda.

The water witch threw her head back. The gills on her cheeks opened wide and the shrieking was renewed with force. From where he stood, pressed flat against the rock face, Ridley could see past the water witch to Mayuri who was leaping up and down and pointing frantically at Ridley. He couldn't hear what Mayuri was trying to tell him because the shrieking of the fearsome creature blocked out all other sounds.

The cardboard box that looked like Chinese food take-out began to vibrate in his hands and the movement helped him realize that Mayuri was trying to tell him to use the pink and yellow caterpillars. By the time Ridley had unfolded the flaps on the box top, the whole thing was shaking violently. The caterpillars were crawling all over one another at a frantic speed. It was as if they had been awakened by the shrieking of the water witch.

Ridley scooped out the caterpillars. He had to drop the box because he needed both hands just to hold onto the fast-moving things. He looked at Mayuri, hoping for some direction as to what he should do next.

The young girl was gesturing wildly. She looked as if she were pretending to throw a baseball. *Throw them?* Ridley thought. *I hope this girl knows what she is doing, or I am dead where I stand!* He threw the handful of fuzzy pink and yellow caterpillars at the water witch as hard as he could. Two hit her in the head and the other three hit her body on the shoulders and chest. But the caterpillars did not bounce off or fall down into the water. They stuck where they hit the creature as if they had been coated with glue. And what happened next was truly the most amazing thing Ridley had ever seen in his whole life.

As the water witch thrashed and shrieked, the caterpillars wriggled and burrowed under a thin layer of her scales. During the metamorphosis of a caterpillar into a butterfly, the caterpillar grows a chrysalis and inside, the physical characteristics of a butterfly grow to replace it. When the butterfly is ready, it forces itself out of the chrysalis. Then the wings slowly expand and harden over the course of twenty-four hours. Only then can the insect fly. Ridley watched this same metamorphosis occur to his pink and yellow caterpillars, only for them, they formed their chrysalises quickly and within milliseconds, butterflies burst out of the scales and large wings the size of Ridley's hands unfolded.

These wings were covered in bright, multicolored designs. They began to flap, slowly at first, but then with a quickening pace. Still attached to the water witch, the butterflies began to lift into the air, pulling her up out of the water. The witch thrashed and shrieked in an angry effort to escape, but the butterflies' bodies were embedded into her

Chrysalis: the hard cocoon or covering that protects a caterpillar while it changes into a butterfly.

flesh. Before Ridley's eyes, the butterflies lifted the creature up into the air, high above the jungle trees and carried her away, off into the distance.

Ridley stood still for a moment, shocked by what had just happened. But then he heard Mayuri yelling at him. "Go! Go! Now is the time! Before another one comes!"

"Another one?" Ridley couldn't believe what he was hearing. Could there really be more of those shrieking things? That thought got him moving in a hurry.

He scrambled along the wall of the cliff toward the waterfall. There was just enough space behind the falls to step between it and the rocks. Once he was behind the waterfall, the sound of it thundered in his ears, and all around there was a fine mist of water floating in the air. The water droplets refracted sunlight, and he was surrounded by snippets of rainbows.

He walked beneath the arch in the rock and through the passageway. It was as if someone had carved a doorway into another world! Ridley emerged into a beautiful gorge . Surrounding him on all sides were rock cliffs. The air was moist from the waterfall and green mosses and grey lichens were growing on every surface. The surrounding cliffs enclosed a large pond. Its water was clear enough that Ridley could see shadows of fish swimming way down deep. He decided that those shadows were the most beautiful things he'd seen since he left home.

"You get ready down there!" he yelled triumphantly at

 Refract: to change the direction of or separate a wave of energy, like a ray of light.
Gorge: a deep, rocky valley with steep sides.
Lichen: a simple plant, green, grey, or yellow in color, that grows in patches on rocks and trees.

the shadows circling in the water. "I'm Ridley Bluefox! I am a famous fisherman and I am here to catch one of you and take you home!" he grinned and rubbed his hands together with excitement.

CHAPTER 12

RIDLEY WAS SO excited that he ran toward the water without watching where he was going. His foot caught on something and he went flying face first into the moss. He grunted as he hit the ground and then quickly rolled over to see what had tripped him. His breath caught in his throat. It was a skeleton! He sat up in surprise.

"It's true!" Ridley said to himself as he pulled the ancient map of Fortuna Island out of his pocket. He unfolded the paper and spread it out on his lap. He read:

> "The only man to catch such a fish,
> Tears of joy he cried
> So mighty and so many tears,
> He dried right up and died
>
> These fish you seek cannot be caught,
> Your prize for trying will be naught."

The poem was real. It was all true. Right there in front of him was the skeleton of a man. It was lying across the ground, with the foot bones just barely touching the water. The bones had been bleached white by the sun and they were still covered with fishing gear, although now the clothing was ratty and falling apart.

"I wonder what really happened to him?" Ridley asked himself as a shiver of fear rippled through his body. But then a splash from the water made him glance up, and he caught sight of a flying fish gliding through the air. One look at the flying fish and he forgot all about the scary skeleton and the warning in the poem. The fish was breathtaking – just like it was in his dream. It glittered silver and gold in the sunlight before it dove back down into the water and disappeared from view. He scrambled to his feet and ran the rest of the way to the water's edge.

The air in the grotto was chilly, and the cool temperature led Ridley to believe that the pond was fed by a cold water spring somewhere in the earth. He could see the outlines of the fish and because he could tell that he'd have to get his hook down deep, he added a weight to the end of his fishing line. He chose a giant jig ⭕ for the lure and a strong fishing line because some of the fish looked quite big.

Ridley cast his line out into the water. With a splunk the giant jig fell down, down, down to the fish. One or two of the flying fish took interest and swam toward it. A few more fish came to investigate and soon there was a whole school of flying fish gathered around Ridley's lure. He jiggled the fishing pole, trying to get one of the fish interested enough to bite. Instead, the fish began to circle around the lure. Soon other flying fish were attracted to the

⭕ **Jig**: a heavy piece of lead with a hook that is both a sinker and a lure.

commotion and swam into the circular formation. Around and around and around they swam while up above Ridley watched, fascinated by their behavior.

Suddenly, one of the fish broke away from the rest of the school. It raced to the center of the swirling circle of fish and with a great gulp, it swallowed the giant jig. Off it swam at top speed. Ridley braced himself, realizing that this fish must be at least five feet long.

The fish pulled the line out of Ridley's fishing pole at an alarming speed. Ridley leaned back. With a jerk that cracked all of the knuckles in his hands, the line finally ran out. He hung onto the fishing pole, but that flying fish gave an awful tug. Ridley ran down the bank of the pond, his legs barreling along beneath him, as he and his fishing pole were pulled by the flying fish. He spied a pile of rocks just ahead and decided to wedge his foot between two of the bigger stones. Positioning one foot between the rocks and the other foot behind him, he lunged backward and got ready to fight his fish. He leaned and pulled hard on the pole.

A slow smile spread across his face as the fish began to slow down, just as Ridley knew it would. But then he realized that the flying fish was only swimming in a large circle back toward Ridley. Once the fish completed his circle, it turned fast in the water and like a bullet, it was off again. Ridley could not hold out any longer, but he wasn't ready to let go.

Ridley screamed and with that, both the fishing pole

and the fisherman who wouldn't let go were pulled into the water with a giant splash.

Down, down Ridley sank to the bottom of the pond. The fish had scattered out of the circular formation and now they swam slowly toward his body. They were all huge fish, the size of himself or larger. Ridley blinked his eyes rapidly and struggled to move, but the water felt heavy. He started to panic as the syrupy liquid flooded into his mouth.

"Don't hold your breath," he heard a voice say. "Try to relax. Relaxing will help you to breathe." Ridley had no idea where the voice was coming from, but he decided to listen. His lungs were starting to fill up with the strange water and he was afraid he was going to drown. After a few seconds of panic, Ridley realized that he could actually breathe. He wondered how that was possible. He heard the same voice answer. "This is a magical place that does not follow the physical rules of your world."

Ridley couldn't figure out whose voice he was hearing and then he heard it again. "We can read your mind, and we are talking by sending you messages with our minds. This is how we communicate."

"But who are you?" Ridley thought.

"We are who you have come here to find. We are the flying fish of Fortune Falls." And as he heard this message, Ridley came to the full realization that he was communicating with the large silver and gold fish that were swimming all around him. He felt small in comparison to some of the flying fish, and he wondered if he was safe.

"Yes, you are safe here, Ridley Bluefox. The grotto of the flying fish is the safest place in the world. You can swim here … forever," the fish voice answered. It sounded like a big group of people all saying the same thing at the same time. It was one voice and yet it was the sound of many.

"This is crazy," thought Ridley. "I must be having another bug dream or something."

"No, this is real," the voice answered back.

"Okay, okay, I'm here at the bottom of the grotto, breathing underwater through some sort of thick syrup that looks like water, but isn't, talking to a bunch of fish with my mind. I guess I may as well feel what it is like to swim around down here, before I catch one of you and get out!" Ridley thought.

"Yes, yes. You are here to swim. That is what you are here to do," the multi-voice in his head intoned. "Come and swim with us, Ridley. We will show you how wonderful it is to live underwater." The multi-voice was slow and hypnotic. It rang through his head making Ridley feel drowsy. His arms and legs began to feel heavy. He floated lazily through the syrupy water.

"Swim, Ridley Bluefox," the voice rang through his head again. "Swim with us."

"You will not catch a flying fish," the voices intoned.

"I will not catch a flying fish," Ridley repeated.

"You will become a flying fish."

"I will become a flying fish," Ridley slurred.

He reached out a hand to touch one of the beautiful fish.

"Hey ... wait a minute!" Ridley tried to speak, but his words were a little slurred. "What's happening?"

"Now it is your turn, Ridley. How does it feel? Those caterpillars weren't bait. They were a lure. A lure we used on you to get you to Fortune Falls. Now *you* are the one who is going to be caught!" The last sentence sunk into Ridley's brain and shocked him out of his sleepy, hypnotized state. He tried to shake his body awake, struggling to move inside the thick water.

"You're wrong! I'm Ridley Bluefox and I am going to catch one of you! I have come all this way! I went to the library for books and maps, I risked my life in an awful airplane with hamburger man, I met an intimidating adventurer and his butler and cats, I went on boats and planes and trains – I ate a bug, for goodness' sakes! I walked in the heat of the sun and the humidity of the jungle, I raced wild boars, I fought off nasty eels and spiders the size of dinner plates! I faced the water witch with nothing but a box of caterpillars. I am taking home a fish!" Ridley was yelling all of this in his mind.

"You will not take home a fish. You will stay here, Ridley Bluefox. You are done with fishing and will become one of us," the hypnotic voices were trying to control his mind.

"Oh yeah? What do you think you're doing to me?" Ridley yelled out. He looked down at his wrists. They were mottled 🐟 gold and silver. At first he thought the bright scales of the flying fish were reflecting off his skin, but no, his skin was actually changing color! He scrubbed at his arms furiously, but the silver and gold patterns would not come off.

"What is going on?" he cried.

"You will become one of us!" the voices rose up in his head once more.

This couldn't be happening to him. He was Ridley Bluefox, the famous fisherman. He would not be bested by a school of fish, magical or not! Ridley had to stop listening to the voices in his head that were trying to control him. He needed to think about something else, a thought that would be strong enough to block the voices out. Ridley thought about an issue of *Fishin' Fabulous* with his picture on the front cover. He tried to imagine what he was wearing in the picture. He tried thinking about the fact that many people would buy it and about how cool he would sound in the interview. But it just wasn't working. The scales growing on his arms were really scaring him, and the voices were getting into his mind anyway.

"This is a very powerful place, here in the grotto behind Fortune Falls," the hypnotic voices penetrated through again. "We live here, protected by the water witch that we let you defeat. We were all once like you. Now you too know the secret of Fortune Falls, Ridley Bluefox. We are fish that were all once great fisherman like you. Great fisherman are the easiest to catch because they always fall

🐟 **Mottled**: spotted or blotched with different colors.

for the bait. The only fisherman to ever leave this grotto was a crooked old man. You know this crooked old man, don't you Ridley? That's right, he works for us, finding fishermen all over the world and helping us lure them into our trap. He made a deal with us, Ridley. In order for him to stay out there in your world, he will spend forever, finding us fishermen to catch. But there will be no deal for you Ridley Bluefox. No one has ever escaped the grotto, and you won't be an exception."

Ridley stared at his hands in horror. The gold and silver pattern was spreading across his skin. His fingers were fully webbed and covered in scales. His arms were turning into fins! He looked down at his legs. Already his knees and calves were covered in the silver and gold scales.

He was becoming a flying fish.

CHAPTER 13

THE SILVER AND gold fish scales had spread all across Ridley's body and he was terrified to find that the scales weren't the only change taking place. His stomach was starting to bloat and thicken as the transformation into a flying fish continued. Ridley grabbed his head in his scaly, webbed hands.

"I won't let this happen! I am not just any fisherman! I have caught too many trophies and had too many fishing triumphs to be brought down by these creatures that call themselves fish!" he bellowed into the syrupy water. He looked at his hands again. The conversion into fins was almost complete.

He had to make another effort to block out the voices or he wasn't going to survive! He needed something powerful to think about, something that these fish just wouldn't be able to beat. But what did he have that was that special? And then it hit him – his fish. That is what he had that was powerful! He was a famous fisherman because he was able to catch fish that no one else could catch. His walls were covered in proof of his famous catches. Ridley envisioned those fish in his mind and then began reciting their names. "Pollo Pollo, Puckmouth, Subahohive," he whispered. "Muknot, Water-dingo, Featherback," he said. "Bottleneck, Knuck-knuck, Riverat!" he shouted, and anger welled up inside of him.

It was working. The names of all of his precious catches were exciting enough to block everything else out of his mind. The flying fish were no longer able to hypnotize him and control his thoughts. In a burst of energy, he thrashed out with his fin arms and began to swim away from the school of flying fish.

"You will become a flying fish and live forever in the grotto of Fortune Falls." The fish voices tried to fill his mind, but Ridley wasn't going to let it work.

"Winklighter, Redback, Barrelnose!" he hollered back at them. Kicking his legs furiously, he began to rise up through the syrupy water. It was thick and his hiking boots were heavy, but he poured every ounce of strength he had into getting away.

"Razorbelly! Quilly-fin! One-Eyed Purple Packfin!" Ridley yelled out one last time. "And I'll keep catching those fish all over the world and live out my life on magazine covers, famous because of my brave adventures. You're just lucky that I didn't catch one of you!" he shouted, and with that he burst through the water, hurling himself halfway up onto the bank of the pond. Ridley coughed the liquid out of his lungs and splashed in the shallows. He moved awkwardly with his half transformed body but managed to drag himself all the way out of the water.

He lay back, exhausted, on the bank of the pond for a moment. It didn't take long before his anger subsided. Now that he was out of the trap, he couldn't help but dwell on the fact that he hadn't caught a flying fish. What would everyone think when he came home empty-handed? But never mind that, what was everyone going to say when he came home with fins for arms and gold and silver scales for skin? They would find out that a bunch of fish had gotten the better of him. He lifted up his fin arm to look at the damage.

"*Yesssss!*" Ridley yelled as he sat up. The gold and silver patterns were fading! And the webbing between his fingers had shrunken, not all the way down but at least a bit. Now they were only webbed up to the knuckle, which was an improvement, for sure. He breathed in a big sigh of relief. For a little bit there, he'd been really scared. Not that he had to mention that to anyone when he got home, of course. Ridley glanced at his legs and saw that they were still heavily scaled. He was disappointed until he realized that they were also soaking wet.

"It's the water! It's this place! I have to get out of here!" Ridley cried and scrambled up onto his feet. He fought with his backpack for a minute before he managed to get all the fishing supplies shoved inside (his fishing pole was forever lost in the grotto) and had it securely fastened onto his back. His fin arms were difficult to maneuver. He backed away from the pond and watched as one last flying fish broke through the surface and glided across the water.

"Ridley…" he heard a whisper in his mind. But Ridley just smiled. He had another long list of fish names ready to recite. He took comfort in the fact that once again, he had done something no other fisherman could manage to do. But he paused for a moment and looked at the water. Part of him wanted to stay, to try to catch a flying fish once more and get that magazine cover. Yet he knew that leaving was the only way to survive. He clasped the straps of his backpack with his scaly, webbed hands and turned his back on the flying fish of Fortune Falls. He would choose to live to fish another day.

Ridley ran toward the arch in the rock without looking back. The farther he got from the flying fish, the more the scales sloughed off his skin. A shiver went down his spine as he jumped over the skeleton bones on his way out of the grotto. He didn't stop to check his skin again until he ducked through the arch and emerged out from behind the waterfall. Rubbing his legs and arms, he removed the rest of the scales. Ridley bent down, scooped the scales off the ground, and tucked them into his pocket, just in case he ever wanted proof that he'd really been to the grotto. Other than the scales, all that was left was slight webbing between his fingers. He hoped no one would notice.

As he reappeared from behind Fortune Falls, Mayuri walked from the water pool to meet him. The relief at seeing him come back out of the grotto was plain on her face.

"You did it! You really did it! You survived the grotto!"

Sloughed: to be shed or cast off, like dead tissue or skin.

Mayuri exclaimed in excitement. Ridley looked at the girl, put an arm on her shoulder and said, "I'm Ridley Bluefox. There's a reason why I'm a famous fisherman." Mayuri smiled and asked, "But you have no fish to take home?"

"Nah, they weren't exactly what I was hoping for. But I wouldn't change a moment of this journey. Of course, I'll catch a fish on my next trip, for sure!"

*   *   *

Ridley and Mayuri walked the longer, safer way back to the marketplace and harbor of Pingu Ma. He then bade his new friend goodbye and hopped on a boat bound for Papua New Guinea. Here he put a phone call through to his parents who arranged to have a plane ticket home waiting for him at the airport in Kuala Lumpur.

A few days later, he boarded the plane, happy to get a window seat, but hoping that the flight wasn't full. Maybe no one would sit beside him. He hated being crowded on a plane.

Ridley was disappointed when a middle-aged man with thick glasses and a big bald spot sat down next to him. His unhappiness lifted however, when his new neighbor pulled out a copy of *Fishin' Fabulous* as well as a couple of scientific journals.

Ridley smiled and turned to the man.

"What are you reading?" he asked innocently.

"Hm? Oh, this? The magazine is for fun, some light

pleasure reading, really. The science journals are for work, of course. I have to conduct a seminar on a rare bio-luminescent 🐟 fish called a moonfish, and I want to be prepared. Dr. Schrieder's my name. I'm an ichthyologist, you see. I study fish."

"Really! How interesting." Ridley's smile spread into a grin that took over his whole face. "What is so rare about these moonfish?"

"Well, to be honest, I don't know much about them because only a few scientists have ever actually seen them. They are bioluminescent, so they live below the photic line 🐟 where there is no light. But that's not all. You see, most bioluminescent fish live in the depths of the ocean. Moonfish, however, are the only bioluminescent fish ever discovered that live in fresh water. They are the rarest of the rare," Dr. Schrieder explained.

"You don't say!" Ridley exclaimed. "Well, in that case, let me introduce myself," he said, extending his still slightly webbed hand toward the man. "I'm Ridley Bluefox, a famous fisherman. Perhaps you've heard of me?"

🐟 **Photic line**: the depth of water at which sunlight (enough for photosynthesis) no longer penetrates through.
Bioluminescent: describes an organism that produces light, like a firefly

Searching for [...]

Check out this time-traveling,
reality-bending, swashbuckling novel!

"... Krill has given us the next best thing to a sequel [to Robert Louis Stevenson's ...

The Uncle Duncle Chronicles:
Escape from Treasure Island
by Darren Krill / ISBN: 978-1-897073-31-5

Sage Smiley is going on vacation with his favorite uncle, world-famous explorer Dunkirk Smiley (a.k.a. "Uncle Duncle"), and can use the powers of a magical talisman to go wherever he wants. But the aerial adventure goes awry when Sage's imagination brings them to Robert Louis Stevenson's **Treasure Island**. Together they must free a group of prisoners from the clutches of Long John Silver, lay claim to the glittering chests of pirate treasure, and fight for their very lives. Does Sage have enough courage and craftiness to survive in this land of legends?

"Non-stop fun and action describes this adventure-filled yarn ..."
– CM: Canadian Review of Materials

"[Krill] handles the blend of existing fiction and his own creation beautifully." – Children's Literature

"It's a rollicking adventure ... very exciting, and custom-made to spark the imagination ..." – Edmonton Sun

www.lobsterpress.com